THE GAMER

CURRENCY CONTROL

by Shawn Pryor

illustrated by Francesca Ficorilli

STONE ARCH BOOKS
a capstone imprint

Published by Stone Arch Books, an imprint of Capstone
1710 Roe Crest Drive, North Mankato, Minnesota 56003
capstonepub.com

Library of Congress Cataloging-in-Publication Data
Names: Pryor, Shawn, author. | Ficorilli, Francesca, illustrator.
Title: Currency control / by Shawn Pryor ; illustrated by Francesca Ficorilli.
Description: North Mankato, Minnesota : Stone Arch Books, an imprint
of Capstone, [2022] | Series: The Gamer | Audience: Ages 8–11. | Audience:
Grades 4–6. | Summary: Thirteen-year-old Tyler Morant uses the special device
given him by the Gaming Masters of the Universe to become The Gamer, and
fights evil Cynthia Cyber's latest creation, a monster named Currency, who
is robbing banks to get Cynthia the money she needs to build a machine that
will give her control over the whole human race.
Identifiers: LCCN 2021030709 (print) | LCCN 2021030710 (ebook) | ISBN
9781663977052 (hardcover) | ISBN 9781666330441 (paperback) | ISBN
9781666330458 (pdf)
Subjects: LCSH: Monsters—Juvenile fiction. | Video games—Juvenile fiction.
| Bank robberies—Juvenile fiction. | Heroes—Juvenile fiction. | CYAC:
Monsters—Fiction. | Video games—Fiction. | Bank robberies—Fiction. |
Superheroes—Fiction. | Supervillains—Fiction. | LCGFT: Superhero fiction.
Classification: LCC PZ7.1.P7855 Cu 2022 (print) | LCC PZ7.1.P7855 (ebook) |
DDC 813.6 [Fic]—dc23
LC record available at https://lccn.loc.gov/2021030709
LC ebook record available at https://lccn.loc.gov/2021030710

Designer: Hilary Wacholz

TABLE OF CONTENTS

You may believe that video games and apps are just harmless fun. But in these special places where we play, a hero works to protect us from the dangers that exist in those worlds . . .

Meet **THE GAMER**, defender of Earth and the digital realm!

REAL NAME: Tyler Morant

HERO NAME: The Gamer

AGE: 13

HERO TOOL: Gamer Activation Device, which transforms Tyler into the Gamer

ENEMY: Cynthia Cyber

MISSION: To defeat evil Cynthia Cyber and her wicked digital monsters

CHAPTER 1

CURRENCY BATTLE!

The Gamer is searching for someone in the digital realm.

"A bunch of banks have been robbed," he says. "I know that Cynthia Cyber is behind this."

Suddenly there's a **laser blast**!

CHTOoOOM!!!

The Gamer leaps to avoid the blast!

BOOM!!

Looking up, the hero sees a **monster**. He is large and green. He has four arms.

One of the monster's hands holds a **glowing red globe**. Numbers swirl inside of it.

"Who are you?" asks the Gamer.

"**Currency!**" yells the monster. "Cynthia Cyber made me. I rob banks." Currency holds up the red globe. "With my powers, I stole money from the banks' computers!"

"That money isn't yours!" says the Gamer.

"I'm taking this money to Cynthia," growls Currency. "With it, she'll get the parts she needs!"

"Parts?" the Gamer asks, confused.

"Cynthia is making a supercomputer!" Currency says. "It will **kidnap** every human on Earth!"

"No way!" says the Gamer.

"And Cynthia will put all those humans in her **evil video games**! Earth will be hers!" Currency lets out a big laugh.

The Gamer leaps into action. "Not if I can help it!" he says.

Currency **shoots** a beam from one of his hands!

The beam hits the Gamer!

Suddenly all is **dark**.

CHAPTER 2

SMALL CHANGE

The Gamer wakes up.

The hero feels different. Everything in the digital realm is **huge**.

As the Gamer looks up, he sees Currency. The monster seems to be **one hundred feet tall**!

"What happened to me?" asks the Gamer.

"My shrink ray made you small!"
Currency says. His voice sounds so large
and loud. "And now," Currency adds,
"I'm going to **crush** you!"

Currency tries to stomp the tiny Gamer.
The small hero dives away before the
monster can crush him.

The Gamer **runs away**. "I've got to find a place to hide. I must get back to regular size. And fast!" he says.

"You can't escape, Gamer!" yells Currency. "I'll find you!"

The Gamer finds a small tunnel. He enters it.

Currency can't follow him into the tunnel. "I'll send my **micro monsters** to take care of you!" Currency screams.

He lifts his hand to the digital sky. Energy **crackles** from the monster's hand.

A bunch of tiny and evil robot bulls and bears fall from the sky.

"Find the Gamer and **destroy** him!" yells Currency.

CHAPTER 3

AGAINST BULLS AND BEARS

The Gamer runs through the tunnel.
At the end of the tunnel, the Gamer sees
a **waterfall**.

The waterfall is surrounded by a digital
pond and trees.

"How am I going to get back to normal
size?" the Gamer asks.

He taps his wrist pad, looking for answers.

The wrist pad explains, "In order to grow, you'll need a **POWER-UP**."

The Gamer thinks, *How am I going to get a Power-Up? I'm too small to—*

Before he can finish his thought, the hero hears **rumbling** and **noises** from the tunnel.

"DESTROY THE GAMER! TEAR HIM TO PIECES!" the robot **bulls** and **bears** growl.

They come out of the tunnel and **push** the Gamer into the water.

The robot animals surround the Gamer. Their sharp claws, teeth, and horns are ready to attack.

"Energy sword, activate!" the Gamer yells.

A flash of light stuns the robot beasts as the Gamer's glowing sword appears.

The Gamer grabs the sword and **battles** the beasts.

After a long battle, the Gamer wins the fight.

A flash of light appears! A small box lands in the Gamer's open hand.

The box speaks. "You have beat your enemies. You have earned a **POWER-UP**."

"I did it!" the Gamer says. "Now it's time to turn the tables on Currency."

CHAPTER 4

TURNING THE TABLES

The Gamer holds on to his **POWER-UP**. He runs out of the tunnel to face his enemy.

"Currency! Your army couldn't beat me and neither will you!" yells the Gamer.

The monster laughs. "You may have beat my army. But now I will **squash** you!"

Currency tries to step on the Gamer.

But the hero takes the **POWER-UP** box and smashes it to the ground!

Currency is blown back by the force of the blast.

The Gamer is back to regular size, holding his energy sword.

"Give me the **globe**, Currency!
That money belongs to the people
of Earth," the Gamer says.

"You'll have to take it from me.
And you're not strong enough to do
that!" Currency says.

He pulls out two swords of his own.

The monster and hero clash swords
as they battle each other.

CHAPTER 5

BANKING ON VICTORY!

As the battle goes on, the Gamer's energy sword starts to weaken.

"My sword has taken **too many hits**," says the Gamer.

Currency takes a hard swing at the Gamer's sword.

The hero's sword is **smashed** to pieces.

"Without your sword, you're powerless," says Currency.

"That's what you think. **Power Shield, activate!**" yells the Gamer.

The Gamer's shield appears.

He grabs it with his right hand.
He throws it at the monster.

Currency **ducks** to avoid the shield.
"Ha, you missed me!" he says.

"I wasn't aiming for you," says the Gamer.

The shield loops around the monster. It **knocks** the glowing red globe out of the monster's hand.

"*Noooo*, the money!" Currency screams.

The Gamer leaps to grab the globe. "Got it!"

Currency is **furious**. "I'm going to shrink you so small that no one will ever find you!"

Currency fires a huge shrink ray blast at the Gamer.

The Gamer lifts his shield to block the laser blast.

The laser **bounces** off the shield. The laser blast goes back and hits Currency.

ZAP!!

"No, you can't do this to *meeeeeeeeeeee*!" says Currency. He shrinks down into nothing.

The Gamer is **victorious**!

"Phew, that monster is finally gone! But there's no time to rest," says the Gamer. "I've got to take this globe of money and put it all back where it belongs."

GLOSSARY

activate (AK-tuh-vayt)—to turn on or to become active

digital realm (DIJ-ih-tuhl RELM)—a fictional world created by video games, phone apps, and the internet

furious (FYOOR-ee-uhs)—very angry

laser (LAY-zur)—a narrow, powerful ray of light

powerless (POW-er-lis)—having no strength

rumbling (RUHM-bling)—low, rolling sounds

shrink ray (SHRINGK RAY)—a fictional tool that uses energy to make people or things smaller

supercomputer (SOO-pur-kuhm-pyoo-tur)—the fastest and most powerful computer available

victorious (VIK-tohr-ee-uhs)—having won

TALK ABOUT IT

1. Why did Currency want to steal the money? What do you think he would gain from it?

2. Discuss the reason why the Gamer needed a Power-Up in order to grow back to normal. How did the Gamer get the Power-Up?

WRITE ABOUT IT

1. The Gamer uses a few different items as he works to beat Currency. Which is the most important? Why? Write a paragraph that argues for your choice.

2. The book begins with the Gamer meeting the villain Currency, who was created by Cynthia Cyber. Write a story about how she created the monster.

THE AUTHOR

Shawn Pryor is the creator and co-author of the graphic novel mystery series Cash and Carrie, co-creator and author of the 2019 Glyph-nominated football/drama series Force, and author of *Kentucky Kaiju* and *Diamond Double Play*, from Jake Maddox Sports Stories. In his free time, he enjoys reading, cooking, listening to streaming music playlists, and talking about why Zack from *Mighty Morphin Power Rangers* is the greatest superhero of all time.

THE ILLUSTRATOR

Francesca Ficorilli was born and lives in Rome, Italy. Francesca knew that she wanted to be an artist since she was a child. She was encouraged by her love for animation and her mother's passion for fine arts. After earning a degree in animation, Francesca started working as a freelance animator and illustrator. She finds inspirations for her illustrations in every corner of the world.